JUST A NORMAL BOY – COMPLETE FICTION (ALMOST)

Two Short Tales

Petrina McGregor

ISBN-13: 9798856192659
ISBN-10: 1477123456

Cover design by: Art Painter
Library of Congress Control Number: 2018675309
Printed in the United States of America

For Robert. Jack. Lizzie. My normal family.

CONTENTS

Just a Normal Boy
Complete Fiction (Almost)

A short story by Petrina McGregor

CHAPTER 1

My seven-year-old knocked himself unconscious. He had leapt off the back of the sofa, straight into a solid wall. His friend explained: "He was trying to jump into the void between two parallel universes."

I gaped at the children.

His friend continued: "He was being Dr Who."

He had been to hospital before – when he was a toddler. Social services were called. I had found an empty bottle of cough mixture on the floor next to the boychild, who was licking his lips appreciatively. I'd been careless with the lid; I hadn't replaced it properly after dosing myself up in the middle of the night. On-call doctors rang the poisons unit at Guy's Hospital, who advised them to keep him under observation for three hours. Drowsiness would trigger emergency protocols.

My boy upended chairs, emptied boxes of toys, tipped over a water dispenser, escaped into a corridor and tripped up a nurse.

Was his behaviour a symptom of ADHD? A result of too much sugar and processed foods? Was it the cough mixture? Or was it him?

*

We could not stand our terraced house in Surrey for another minute. It looked out over a Waitrose car park with an awkward, hairpin entrance. Angry Range Rover drivers would lean out of their cars and yell at each other, hooting furiously, right there on our doorstep. Plus, a damp patch, the shape of Alaska, crept in from the roof. The builder charged thousands, which we had to borrow. Alaska reappeared soon after the work was finished. The builder did not answer any of my calls. Emails to him went unanswered. Perhaps he made it into the void between two parallel universes.

"Let's move to Devon," I suggested, craving a house that was free of damp and far away from road rage hotspots.

Because I worked part time, it became my task to scan Devon's teaching vacancies as soon as they were published. I helped draft an application for anything that looked promising. I had my husband's CV and a generic application letter on file so that by the time he came home in the evening, all he had to do was proofread and press send.

We had lousy wi-fi – probably some complication caused by Alaska. The screen froze. I controlled the urge to scream and smash things. I went to make tea instead. By the time I got back, the screen would no longer be frozen, I promised myself.

It was still frozen on a webpage advertising teaching jobs abroad.

I jiggled the mouse. Sipped my tea.

Stared at the screen. Unfreeze, stupid bloody thing! Why the hell would I want to apply for a teaching job in Rome?

Actually, why wouldn't I?

The screen unfroze. I topped and tailed his letter. Sent it off. Didn't mention it to my husband.

When he was invited for interview, he yelled at me: "Do you need a map? Rome is not in Devon!"

He got the job. We went to Rome.

*

Is it true that ADHD runs in families? Is ADHD associated with impulsivity? Am I impulsive? Are ADHD kids often creative? There is a new word out there about the condition: 'lighthousing'. Also known as hyperfocus. Concentration on one thing to the exclusion of all else, but that beam of brilliant focus is not always active. Until the lighthouse is switched on, thoughts ping about like grasshoppers.

*

Rome. August. The heat felt like a living presence breathing fire over us. Our house was on a hillside overlooking an olive grove. Horses dawdled in amongst the olive trees, lazily swooshing their tails at flies, cropping at grass. I burst into tears when I first saw it.

The boychild couldn't sleep. He'd never encountered such heat. In the end, we draped damp towels over him in his bed.

On our first morning, it was already hot at seven o'clock. Moments earlier, I was awoken by our bedroom door bumping open and my son's bare feet padding towards my bed. Tousled and rubbing his eyes, he clambered up to say hello to us. We were instructed to greet his teddy. The bedraggled bear was shoved into our faces; I kissed its plastic nose and solemnly asked Bearness how he was.

The boychild watched my sleepy conversation with Bearness, assessing the traditional game in this new place. He seemed to be relieved that this was one thing that had not changed. From the time he was big enough to walk, he had always wandered in and woken us up early. The first drink of the day was taken together while the previous night's dreams were discussed.

My husband and I waited to see who would be more desperate for caffeine. Climbing off the bed would be an act of surrender: it would involve making the tea and clearing up the chaos from last night's supper.

I won. He got the tea. Dirty dishes clattered noisily into the sink downstairs. A cry of disgust. Something had been left out and putrefied in the heat. I pretended not to hear.

The boychild sat still and intent – senses on high alert – trying to decide if Italy was terrible. It was his first morning in his new home.

Everything he had ever known was still boxed up. Even the air smelt different to Surrey: fresh, dewy, with a tang of freshly watered mint wafting in from a neighbour's garden. The early morning light was wrong. It was too golden. Not terrible, but the strangeness of it jolted him. The birds sounded odd, too. A long tweet that sounded crackly, like old-fashioned radio static, drawn out, a slow glissando down through two or three notes. "Are those birds electric?" he asked.

Anything was possible here, as far as he was concerned.

He'd been furious when we told him that we would move away from the damp house overlooking the car park. To him, that noisy, mouldy universe was perfect. The damp patch was a Disney Pixar beast shapeshifting between the plaster and the wallpaper. He was slightly mollified when he was told that he would go on an aeroplane.

*

The history teacher at the international school asked me to write a play about Lupercal. She planned to take Year Seven off timetable one afternoon to re-enact Ancient Roman festivals. I discovered that Lupercal got pretty wild in Ancient Rome. My script would have to tread a cautious line between innocent students' sensibilities and stories of raucous, semi-naked partying.
While writing the script late one night, a dreadful ache spread from my lower back round to my belly. It felt like clawed hands were twisting and squeezing hard. I'd been hoping I was pregnant. I wanted a little Italian baby. I would name her Flavia, my flame child, a wild thing. She would be little and dark haired, to complement the long-limbed blondie I'd already produced. The cramps intensified. Flavia drained away. I did not tell anyone. It happened so early. I had not even had time to buy a pregnancy test. But I was pretty sure that I had felt her fierce little spirit trying to grow in me.

The boychild looked anxiously at my face as I hunched over the steering wheel on the way to school. I was still cramping up as the miscarriage ran its course.
"You're going the wrong way, Mama."

Aged six, he took charge of navigation. While I negotiated the espresso-fuelled drivers, the boychild's hyperfocus on the map calmed me enough to get us to school. The drive could take more than an hour, on winding roads. No wonder Flavia found my womb too uncomfortable: a tight, tense, dark space deep inside me. I clenched the steering wheel, gritted my teeth and swore.

*

One of the primary school music teachers, a colleague of my husband's, said that my boychild was gifted. What the kid didn't know, he improvised. He flipped from the trumpet to the keyboards to the guitar with ease. He would be performing Boney M's famous Christmas hit in the carol concert. On the night, the boychild stood at the front of the church with an electric guitar. Three other frightened-looking small boys joined him: keyboard, drums and bass. They started out of sync, then stopped raggedly. The band huddled; panicky whispering. The audience grew restless. Suddenly they made a decision.

"Two, three four. . ."

They slammed out Highway to Hell.

The nativity play children in the front row went wild. The little girl who was cast as the Virgin Mary danced about savagely, swinging a baby Jesus doll by one arm.

*

Some say that people with ADHD often act inappropriately. They are annoying, tactless and impulsive. They say that children are labelled as having ADHD when they are simply attention seekers who need discipline and an orderly home life. Parents dose them up with drugs to make them easier to manage.

*

7

Lupercal was imminent. I had learned that Ancient Romans celebrated Lupercal around mid-February, their time for purification. I wondered if it eventually became Valentine's Day. It's referred to in Shakespeare's Julius Caesar: Caesar asks Mark Anthony to race through the forum and bless his barren wife. Caesar believed that she would conceive as a result. Her void would be filled. I watched the black-and-white film, in which the bare-chested young Marlon Brando raced about looking hot and making older wives look flustered before rushing off to get pregnant. I cast a broad-shouldered, hunky drama teacher for this role.

One of my colleagues was hit in the face by my boychild waving a palm frond too excitedly. He had been allowed to attend the festivities, even though he was too young: it was strictly for Year Sevens. Perhaps his class teacher was pleased to have some respite from his antics. A thin strip of blood oozed above the injured teacher's eye.

The hunky drama teacher relished his role, blessing all the female teachers, stroking their heads with his palm frond, which had been spray-painted gold. They all twinkled coquettishly at him. When it was my turn, my chest felt thick and full, clogged with grief for Flavia. I stared unsmiling past him. The boychild noticed and loudly asked why I was not being nice to that man.

*

The headmistress of the primary school summoned me. The boychild had crowned a week of catastrophic failures and forgetfulness by calling his teacher a puttana before running away across the playground.

He had no idea what puttana meant, but still.

Her eyes were cold. She bristled with the special disapproval headteachers reserve for despicable parents. My question: does he have ADHD? No, no, no. She said no to all my questions – three times, eyes half closed, with one decisive head shake and a chopping arm motion, as if she was sweeping my foolishness out of the room.

ADHD is a myth, she said, heavily over-diagnosed. A media frenzy, driven by tabloids. Clinically unproven. What the child needs, she said, is routine. A sensible diet. Help with organisation. Boundaries. Limited screen time. Love.

CHAPTER 2

I read somewhere that people with ADHD often exhibit a lack of empathy and compassion. Studies are being carried out to establish whether there is a link between ADHD and narcissism.

The pendulum in my head swung back: suspicion that my boychild had ADHD was quashed again. He was wild and unpredictable, but narcissistic? No. If only there was some sort of blood test we could do.

*

The headmistress sent me a cold, business-like email. The boychild was in trouble. Again. A meeting was scheduled for lunch time.

He was already sitting in her office, eyes fixed on his shoes, shoulders up.

A tiny squeak from a corner drew all eyes before anyone had the chance to clarify what the meeting was about. In a box sat a tiny black kitten.

The boychild and his friend had found her two days earlier, along with her bedraggled little brother, in a plastic bag. The kittens had been dumped on the street outside the friend's house. They'd convinced his friend's mother to keep the male kitten; my boy kept the female. The mother did not discuss the situation with me. Something to do with the language barrier, perhaps. The boychild's Italian was a lot better than mine.

The kittens needed feeding every few hours. His friend's mum had told him that they were only about two weeks old. She gave my son a specially adapted bottle and kitten milk. Because she needed such frequent feeding, he had been sneaking the kitten into school and back home.

Had I really not noticed a kitten in my car? Two days in a row? The headteacher pursed her lips. She tried to disguise an eyeroll by sweeping a non-existent strand of hair from her forehead.

He was caught when he left the kitten wrapped in a towel in his teacher's filing cabinet. He'd decided that he would go mad if caring for her would make him miss his lunchtime kickabout with a football. Usually, the teacher did not go into her classroom during breaks, so he could stash the kitten there. Unluckily, the teacher did not stick to her usual routine that day.

The kitten had shat all over a set of unmarked tests before squealing to be let out. My joke about the accuracy of the kitten's assessment of the work was met with silence. Impulse control, I told myself. Impulse control.

It was agreed that we could not just let the kitten die by leaving her at home to starve. I would somehow have to manage her in the staffroom, alongside teaching. At this point the boychild looked up, relieved. He had been expecting the worst. Aged ten, his faith in humanity was beginning to waiver.

Within months, the kitten had grown and was pregnant. Disapproving cat lovers scolded us: "Why didn't you get her sterilised?"

How would I have guessed that six-month-old kittens could get pregnant?

*

We were watching the football World Cup with a group of teaching families. Beer and Prosecco flowed; a smoky barbecue made the air fill with rich, tangy aromas. A group of kids approached me to plead the boychild's case: he'd been begging to keep the new kittens once they were born. It would be awful to break up her family, they argued, eyes brimming at the idea. Later, I would wonder if it would be poor parenting to go back on my agreement, which had been made under the influence of Prosecco. I had agreed: we'd keep them. Provided one kitten could be named after the first player to score a goal in the World Cup.

Tshabalala was born, along with five siblings.

Weeks later, my husband would need to negotiate his way down the stairs carefully in the mornings, trying not to tread on excited, bouncing kittens. It looked like he was surfing on a sea of cats.

Word soon got out among the feline population that our home was a good place to get a free meal and a bed for the night. A cat house, of sorts. Entitled-looking strays nonchalantly lounged on our sofas and beds. Kittens chased each other up curtains. The sofa was clawed to pieces. A tomcat sauntered in and sprayed his scent all over the television. We would be woken up in the middle of the night by pussy riots as rival males fought for domination.

The boychild sat hollow-eyed in the car after a night of cats screaming at each other. His school uniform stank of tomcat. "How did things get so out of control with the cats?" he asked mournfully. "I just thought it would be nice to keep their family together. They were so sweet when they were tiny."

I gripped the steering wheel, thinking, this is all down to you, kiddo. "Can we get a dog?" he asked.

Absolutely no, a thousand times no.

House Rules:

1. No strays!
2. Doors and windows to be kept closed at all times. (See Rule 1.)
3. Water pistols are to be kept loaded in strategic places around the house at all times. (Also, see Rule 1.)
4. No cat food left in bowls after REGULAR feeding times.

5. No kittens! All kittens to be sterilised, vaccinated and re-homed.

The new regime was notable for its failures. Tshabalala could not be re-homed; we were stuck with her and her mother. Their mischief increased in proportion to the decrease in strays and kittens. They regularly scampered from the kitchen with our dinner in their jaws. One evening, Tshabalala dragged a neighbour's cold roasted turkey into our garden. The turkey was larger than Tshabalala, but her determination could move mountains.

I sat in a friend's sunny garden entertaining her with cat anecdotes. "It's just that this whole thing started with the boychild's impulsivity," I complained. A segue into my ADHD rant. His grades were slipping. Books were lost, kit was forgotten, homework went missing. How would he cope in secondary school in a few years?

My friend told me, "Henry, that monster in the primary school, is ADHD. When you compare your boy—"

Henry's hell-raising was almost as famous as that of our cats, but he lacked their charm. He had a pinched face, flashing eyes and a mean streak that could clear the playground. He was constantly snatching, taunting, hitting, stealing, breaking, overturning. A blur, racing around classrooms, under tables, over chairs. A human tornado.

My boychild was nothing like Henry. Yes, he could be inattentive, fizzing with energy, unpredictable, impulsive. But also compassionate, fun and warm.

My friend smiled at the children rampaging on an elaborate climbing frame nearby. To them, adults no longer existed as they conquered dragons and flew over battlements.

She said, "I found an article about Omega 3 for you. It boosts concentration."

I was hearing more and more that this was the new miracle drug, supporting brain development, aiding focus. Could this, with even more support from home, be the answer?

"I'm going to add to our house rules. I need to help him with organisation. Hopefully, he'll stop losing stuff, forgetting homework. . ."

"He's just a normal boy," she reassured me.

CHAPTER 3

My husband's first wife is coming to Rome.

Anxiety has been gnawing at me in dreams every night. I jolt awake at around two most mornings. Waves of her hatred pulsate towards me in the darkness.

A decade ago, when my husband and I first met, he was employed as a peripatetic music teacher at the school where I was working. He had drifted into the staff room, glamorously silver haired and bohemian – a cool, relaxed contrast to my exhausted, frazzled colleagues. He had time for wisecracks. The twinkle in his eyes had not been extinguished by the relentless demands working in a busy London comp .

He was a professional musician, conducting a small orchestra. It paid badly; the job at our school was intended to boost his income while his wife was trying to make it as an opera singer. By the time I discovered that he had a wife, it was too late. I was in love with him.

Adulterer. A horrible word, laden with Old Testament guarantees of hellfire and righteous, stone-throwing old men.

He had been married to her for a decade. They didn't have any children. When she eventually found out about us, her rage was appalling. She swept into my little studio flat, shrieking, smashing things. My husband – or her husband, as he was at the time – sat there, aghast as she cried and smashed my stuff. While my flat was being wrecked, he withdrew as if trying to make himself invisible. He stared into a small space he seemed to have created around him.

Afterwards, I wondered if he would have stopped her if she had taken a carving knife to my throat.

15

She paused long enough to register my swollen belly, pregnant with the boychild. She stopped smashing and screaming. I was tempted to tell people afterwards that she acted like an evil fairy casting a spell, pointing at my belly, head thrown back, exclaiming, "So! That's what this is all about!"

In truth, she crumpled. Her pain and defeat were more horrible to witness than her tantrum.

If I hadn't been pregnant, I would have left him out of pure shame, but I didn't have the courage to raise a child on my own. The shame grew and wrapped itself around me like a python as I processed the horror of what I'd – of what we'd – done to her.

He wilted in the face of her wrath. Each day he aged and shrivelled a little more. The snap and spark in him that I'd found irresistible was snuffed out. He wrinkled like an old apple when each new catastrophe was unveiled in the divorce settlement. Their home went to her, and most of his meagre savings. Guilt prevented him from arguing. He stopped looking me in the eye.

I'd changed from being wildly desirable to the root of his abject disgrace. We tottered under the weight of our combined guilt. The prospect of a baby filled us with terror, but my terror of raising a child alone was worse. We clung together, not liking each other very much.

We trudged from bank to bank and pleaded for a mortgage. Finally, we were lent enough to move into the house with the damp patch. Suddenly, I was a grown-up. My twenties ended, and I was pregnant, mortgaged, and married to a man two decades older than me.

*

My parents were disgusted. I was going to end up just like my grandmother, they muttered. Their warning mystified me. My slightly dotty grandmother was far more contented than they had ever been. Ending up like her would not be a bad outcome. Still, my parents refused to attend the wedding ceremony in the registry office.

Even so, breaking the news to my family was not as dramatic as my husband's first wife discovering our affair. But the experience had left me feeling stranded.

Days earlier, I had taken a deep breath, picked up the phone, and arranged a visit at a time when I was sure that my mother and my grandmother would be together.

I approached my grandmother's house. Her garden was ablaze with roses. Boughs, higher than my head, were weighed down by blooms in every shade of yellow: lemon, sunflower, butter, gold. Their sweet perfume filled the lane.

My grandmother's front door flung the front door open, her face glowing with joy, arms open wide, welcoming me. For a moment, I felt safe.

My mother did not come to the door. She sat bolt upright on the edge of a hard wooden chair. She clutched a walking stick with a brass handle, ready to wave it threateningly at my grandmother's terriers if they ventured too close. On a table next to her was a glass of water, a packet hay fever tablets, and a box of tissues.

My mother greeted me with a single nod, imperiously holding up a hand, warning me not to hug her.

"Bad back," she explained.

Mother's complexion was ruddier than usual today and her grey hair looked dry and scratchy: the result of yet another unsuccessful home perm. The knuckles of her hands stuck sharply up as she gripped the walking stick. She narrowed her flinty eyes at me; two vertical lines deepened between her eyebrows.

I was quickly distracted from my mother's habitual greeting. My grandmother, still with her arm around me, propelled me into her kitchen – a mess of pots and pans on every surface. She released me long enough to press a wineglass filled with Prosecco into my hand.

Before I could get a word in, my grandmother launched into her anti-champagne flute protest: "Can't bear those stupid, tall, skinny glasses that are so fashionable now. They're never big enough. Prefer the old-fashioned ones, the fat round ones. Did you know that they were designed to be the same shape as Marie-Antoinette's boobs?"

A loud sigh could be heard from my mother in the front room, where she had remained. My mother had mastered the art of audible, disapproving sighs. She probably had not moved, except to wave her stick to warn the dogs to keep away.

I was steered back into the front room. My grandmother threw herself into a squashy armchair, propped her feet up and threw a cushion at me. Normally, I would make myself comfortable on the floor so that the dogs are within easy reach. This time, I stood awkwardly, cuddling the cushion and using it as a shield to hide my belly. They had not noticed yet.

I explained that I had better not drink the Prosecco.

My mother looked at me with hope in her eyes. She had spent my adult life wishing that I would be more sensible, more austere.

I looked away from her and focused on my grandmother. I took a deep breath. "I'm going to have a baby."

I took the precaution of phrasing it like that. If I'd said that I was pregnant, my mother would have started researching abortion clinics.

In all fairness, my mother's start in life had been challenging. She was the result of an unexpected pregnancy. In those days, a fatherless child attracted much bitchy speculation and gossip. Her childhood had been dogged by cruel jibes.

She hated visiting the small seaside town with a tight-knit community of busybodies where my grandmother still lived to this day. When my mother had been a little girl, many people had shrugged and left them alone; but just as many would not let their children play with "that illegitimate child". Either way, my mother was an outcast.

And now, my mother declared, I was going to inflict a similar fate on my own baby.

Her outrage increased when I explained that I would be getting married – just as soon as the divorce came through.

Intense respectability was my mother's defence against being the talk of a 1960s small town. She wore that respectability the way most people wear their finest clothes to the smartest parties. She suspected that my grandmother and I were determined to ruin her image of wholesome goodness.

She stared at me through flinty eyes as she processed the words "divorce" and "baby". My grandmother sipped her Prosecco, caressing one of the dogs with a toe.

Weighing up my latest list of evils, my mother decided that abortion was surely less scandalous than causing a divorce and an unplanned pregnancy.

Still, she tried to convince me that a termination was my only option. Better that than being saddled to a musician – she had demanded to know what "the father's" job was before bothering to find out his name and whether we loved each other. A divorced musician!

During this conversation, my grandmother stood up, hugged me, then made tea which she pressed into my hands. It warmed me a little from the icy disapproval that radiated from my mother.

I loved my grandmother for being so kind, but the love that I felt for the boy growing inside me was a powerful enchantment against my mother's bitterness.

My husband's parents, however, seemed to warm to me. Perhaps they disliked my predecessor.

The First Wife had steadfastly refused to have his children. This news came as a relief. I clung to that fact hoping that some absolution could be found for me in it. But I wondered later if she had some eerie foreknowledge that a child would cause him to unravel. Although he adored the boychild, he crumbled in the face of the child's relentless, fizzing energy. When my husband wasn't doting on the baby, he quivered with anxiety: wasn't it too soon to stop breastfeeding? Shouldn't I be exposing him to music that was a little more highbrow than Nellie the Elephant? Why was I not wrapping him up against the cold?

The Christmas before we went to Rome, the First Wife seemed to be forgotten. My husband and I were tentatively becoming friends once more. At times, we felt quite fond of each other.

But then an invitation came to watch Her singing in Handel's Messiah at a prestigious location in London.

Divorce suited her. Her career was taking flight: she was being invited to perform with renowned artists throughout Britain, and there were whispers of work in New York.

She was dazzling as the soprano soloist in The Messiah. She had lost weight and dyed her hair flame red. She towered over me when she came to speak to us afterwards, oozing charm and magnanimity. Churlishly, I suspected that she was enjoying the fact that I'd never lost my podgy post-pregnancy figure; I had a cheap haircut and a chalky complexion. That her ex-husband had visibly aged seemed to add a gleam to her kohl-ringed eyes. We'd got what we deserved: poverty, exhaustion and ignominy.

And now, almost five years later, she was coming back to haunt us yet again. She had been invited to perform at some swanky location in Rome. She wasted no time informing her ex-husband that she was on her way.

I wished she would leave us alone. Seeing her twice every ten years was too much.

One night before her arrival, I lay in bed, miserably watching the black square of the window, waiting for it to turn grey with the coming dawn. Thoughts sparked about in my head. A vicious inner voice hissed that his First Wife was smarter, more exciting, less chaotic. Of course, it hissed, he still loves Her.

The previous evening, out of the corner of my eye, I could see my husband's shoulders droop because I remained silent about his assessment of some highbrow song on the radio. I knew nothing about opera. The memory of a screaming opera singer smashing up my flat had put a dampener on any flicker of interest.

Insomnia now had me pacing around the dark living room, agonising about the First Wife's impending visit. At last, exhaustion chased me back to bed. My mind was still leaping about, but my leaden limbs cried out for sleep.

I fantasised about making a fool of her. My tense muscles began to soften slightly as the details of my imaginary one-upmanship took shape.

She would visit our school, having been invited to give a lecture to a handful of specially selected talented young musicians. Of course, my gifted boychild would be part of the elite group chosen from the primary school. They would cluster around her in the music room, listening politely but disinterestedly to her self-admiring, patronising lecture about how to become an opera singer.

A sensation of floating washed over my knotted muscles as the picture took shape. Half dream, half fantasy, the scene wrote itself in my mind. The First Wife would perform for the primary school group, shrieking her way through Queen of the Night, missing notes.

The polite children would try not to wince. She'd bow gracefully at the end of the performance to a smattering of applause. My boychild's hand would shoot up afterwards.

"I liked that Queen of the Night thingy that you sang," he'd begin. I could visualise her smugly cocking a perfectly stencilled eyebrow.

"But," the boychild would continue, "I think there was a bit that went wrong."

The First Wife would freeze.

"I don't think so, dear," the First Wife would say condescendingly, showing her teeth in a snarling smile. "I've been perfecting that piece for decades, and I hardly think that an eight-year-old -"
"I'm ten," the boychild would interrupt, impatiently scrambling to his feet.

He'd march to the piano, miraculously picking out the tune with virtuoso skill.

"At this bit," he'd announce to her, "you went off-key." My dream-child would replay the tune, replicating her bum notes midway through.
"I just thought you should know." He'd run through it once again, note-perfect, embellished with chords and trills. Mozart reincarnated.

The dream audience and the primary school music teacher would be thunderstruck: the boychild would be absolutely correct, displaying a talent that was stupendous. The notes that he'd picked out on the piano would precisely echo the First Wife's rendition, skittering off-key.

When the identity of the precocious little genius was finally revealed to the First Wife, I half-imagined, half-dreamed her transforming into a wicked fairy in a puff of acrid green smoke, exclaiming, "Cursed be that child!"

I fantasised about her sweeping out of the school, refusing to perform to the secondary school choir. The teachers in the staff room would snigger about her and clap me on the back, telling me that I had saved my husband from a lifetime of misery at the hands of an egotistical prima donna.

I was smiling in my sleep when the boychild shook me awake. I had not heard him opening my bedroom door. He was urgently asking me if snails are dangerous. Blearily, I blinked at him. "Mama!" he repeated, shaking me rather roughly. "What if one of those giant African giant snails got into a fight with a small snake?"

"Depends," I stalled croakily.

"A baby black mamba," he said, barely containing his impatience.

"How baby?" The boychild held his fingers five inches apart, then used his thumb and forefinger to demonstrate the spindly girth of the black mamba.

"Still think the mamba wins," I croaked. "It's got poison. And speed."

The boychild scowled. He was clearly rooting for the giant African snail. "But—"

I stopped him, holding up an imperious hand. "Tea," I croaked. "Can't think until tea. . ."

"Adults are useless," grumbled the boychild, kicking the bedside. "They never talk about anything interesting. All they want is tea."

This was true, I reflected. No first wives. No insomnia. No horrible tussles between mambas and giant snails. Just tea.

*

When the day came to watch the First Wife's performance in Rome, I pretended to have a migraine. I lay on the bed in a darkened room, groaning. My husband, flustered, arranged for the boychild to spend the night with a friend.

As soon as his car sped away towards the concert venue, silence settled over the house. The temperature dropped. I might as well have been in outer space; the house had become so cold and silent.

I'd wished for a quiet day to myself for so long. Now that I had it, I hated it.

An hour passed. I picked up a book and found myself reading the same page over and over, wondering what I had just read. I tried to doze. I climbed out of bed and made myself some lunch, which I couldn't eat. It ended up in a Tupperware box, ready to be refrigerated. I switched on the radio, only to be bombarded with opera music. I snapped it off.

A ping came from my phone. I grabbed it gratefully.

A text from the art teacher at school came. A group of colleagues were planning a night out, not far from where I lived. Would I like to join them?

I sent blessings her way. She had never stopped inviting me, even though I had declined every invitation for months, so swamped had I been in schoolwork and caring for the boychild.

I raced to the shower, suddenly energised. Why shouldn't I join them? I could have just one drink, then collect the boychild the next morning, as agreed. My husband need never know. If he could justify going to see the First Wife, I could defend a tiny fib and one quick drink with my friends.

*

Before my eyes opened the next morning, the pain of a brutal hangover woke me up. Nausea brewed ominously in my throat.

I groped futilely for my phone. One eye opened. It felt as if a punishment for lying about having a migraine the previous day was now being inflicted on me: light sliced into my half-open eye like a blade, cutting deep into my brain. Pain rippled through my skull and down the back of my neck. The nausea bubbled up.

Where the hell was I?

Bathroom. Needed a bathroom, quick.

The apartment I was in was small. I staggered to the bathroom, one hand on the wall which seemed to sway, as if we were at sea.

After I had been sick, I curled up on the floor of the bathroom. In came the art teacher with her flatmate, bearing paracetamol and coffee. So, I was in their apartment. Relief was short-lived: the smell of the coffee sent me crawling back to the toilet, retching and heaving.

Self-loathing washed over me. I was supposed to be a respectable mother, sensible, organised. Here I was, behaving like a gap year student. At least all my clothes were still on.

Eyes watering, I clung to the wash basin and rinsed out my mouth. My friends rubbed my back. I did not deserve such compassion.

I remembered the night in a series of snapshots: a long, slurred rant about my husband going running to his glamorous ex every time she snapped her fingers. The hunky drama teacher, a self-admiring rake whom I couldn't stand normally, was unexpectedly kind. He assured me that I was ten times cleverer and nicer than that raddled old opera singer. Later, I'd been dancing and singing noisily in the street with my friends. We swayed and chanted football anthems on the way to someone's apartment. An angry face appeared at a window, roaring at us in Italian. We jeered and pulled two fingers. The science teacher tripped over a bin. More jeers. A tangle of bodies: we kept falling over as we tried to help him to his feet.

I hadn't laughed until my sides ached in such a long time.

Leaning on the washbasin, I croaked: "The boychild. Have to collect him."

Then came the icy horror of realising that my husband would be at home, wondering where I was. My phone. I reeled about the apartment in a panicky haze of queasiness, wincing at the headache.

My phone was nowhere to be found. I must have lost it somewhere the previous night.

The hunky drama teacher strolled into the lounge wearing nothing but a pair of boxer shorts. The art teacher's flatmate, the only sober one there, leapt for her hijab and hastily covered her hair. I looked at her, trying to communicate telepathically: Where had he appeared from? Had he been here all night?

The hunky drama teacher grinned at me, moving in too close. Could he smell the puke? I put my hand over my mouth and edged away, quickly averting my eyes from his torso. Why the hell couldn't he wear a shirt? He asked how I was feeling.

Sick. Very sick. Scared, scared, scared. What have I done? Surely, I'd remember if we'd. . .

*

The art teacher and her flatmate tried to help with damage limitation. They shooed the hunky drama teacher out, fed up with him parading his tanned, ripped abs. They assured me that no matter how inebriated I was, I would never do anything as stupid as getting involved with him. There was drunkenness, then there was insanity.

They admitted they'd had a fleeting moment of anxiety the previous night, watching him giving me a too-long hug as I ranted about the First Wife, but I'd quickly been distracted by the singing, dancing and fun.

They helped me collect the boychild and then drove us both home. I wondered how I would explain my absence to my husband. Perhaps I should just tell him the truth – admit to him that the First Wife's hold over him made me miserable.

The house was in silence when I arrived. My husband's car was parked out front.

I eased myself quietly through the front door. The boychild burst in, shattering any prospect of a stealthy entry. He roared through the house, excitedly searching for his dad. He'd had a brilliant evening and wanted to tell his dad all about toasted marshmallows, midnight swims, and sparklers in his friend's garden.

My husband was glowing, sipping coffee, and listening attentively to the boychild, relishing his son's delight. When had I last seen my husband look so contented?

"The performance was sublime!" He gushed when our son ran out of news and scampered off to investigate the whereabouts of his nerf gun. Had my husband noticed that I had been out all night? That I reeked of stale alcohol? He hadn't really looked at me properly at all. His eyes seemed to be fixed in the middle distance, on the glittering phantom of the First Wife.

He continued, "Afterwards, she invited me to dinner with the performers. And I've got the most amazing news. I've been offered a job interview! Conducting a university choir!"

It was not just any university. The offer was prestigious, the pay decent. "We might be able to escape teaching at last! We could go back home!"

But I liked teaching. I liked Italy. I had friends. Friends who forgave me when I misbehaved.

It dawned on him that I had not said a word yet.

"You poor thing – still suffering with a sore head?" he asked, as if he was seeing me for the first time.
"Mmm. When did you get home?" I asked him.
Confusion made the glow fade from his face. "About half an hour ago. I assumed that you'd popped out to collect…"

Of course. My car was still parked near the bar from last night. He'd expected I'd gone to pick up the boychild from his sleepover, as agreed, when he saw that I wasn't home.
I asked him, "Where did you stay?"
His answer: "Oh, er, yes – they organised a room for me in the hotel where they were all staying. I thought I texted all this to you. . ."
Oh. And I had lost my phone. I quietly asked where exactly he had stayed in the hotel. Had he been with her? In her room?

He erupted. He raved at me, asking why I could not understand how wonderful it was for him to be surrounded by professional musicians, serious artists. Did I not yet realise who he was? The dazzling people with whom he'd once worked? He ranted that he was a Somebody before he met me. Working with talented musicians, true artists. That was all that he had ever wanted.

All?

I was not ready to say it out loud yet. But I had known, almost from the outset, that I would never be enough for him.

Of course he still loved her.

I slunk off. I'd hated the sight of him when he had told me about his hopes for a job offer, reverting to the man he'd been when I first met him: silver haired, sardonic, glamorous. Not mine.

Later, he stalked in, clutching his iPad. He was looking at a social media page. With an angry sweep of the back of his hand, palm up, he gestured at a photo.

Me. A bar. A glass of Prosecco in one hand, the other cradling the hunky drama teacher's neck.

The next photo. I was no longer centre stage. But in the bottom left of the picture, the hunky drama teacher had his arm around me possessively. His mouth seemed to be pressed to the side of my head. I knew that he'd been telling a joke, but it looked terrible. It looked like he was kissing me.

The next photo. Me dancing in the street. No hint of a migraine.

My husband climbed into the car and drove away. Before he went, he called me a cheat and a liar.

The boychild had been listening to the tirade. Anxiously, he crawled into my arms, tears in his wide eyes.

CHAPTER 4

We limp through the rest of the term, freakishly polite to each other. Animosity throbs below the civil veneer, however. The cats steer clear of us.

Work is a blessing. I stay as late as possible every evening, until my son pleads with me to take him home.

Saturday. I climb out of bed as quietly as I can so that I don't have to speak to my husband. He is pretending to sleep. I can tell from the quietness of his breathing and the tautness of his shoulders that he is tense, hoping that I will go away. I gladly oblige.

The boychild is already downstairs. I hear him fiddling with the TV. The days of him padding in to greet us as soon as he wakes up are over.

The sun is already hot. The air is crisp and golden, even at this early hour on a Saturday morning. The boychild and I decide to eat breakfast in the village.

Towering umbrella pines line the lane outside and offer welcome shade. The tang of resin fills the air as we crunch fallen needles underfoot. I make a mental note to sweep the front patio when we return home. Our neighbour told us that before we moved there, a wildfire had swept across the hillside and straight towards the houses. They had been spared, thanks to fastidious sweeping and watering.

The boychild finds a fallen pinecone – it is the size of his head. He collects them every year, stacking them on the hearth next to the fireplace. Pinecones burn like coal; they can warm up the entire house in the winter.

Once we tried extracting pine nuts from the cones. We quickly became fed up with the laborious task.

Our stroll to the village takes us past a large olive grove which has been fenced in; ragged green sacking has been attached to the fence. I wonder why. Any attempt at privacy is futile – the sacking is not attached high up enough to prevent passers-by from peering in at the attractive, but unspectacular, olive trees. It must have been an attempt to calm the owner's two dogs.

The attempt was unsuccessful.

Eagerly, the boychild peers in as we stroll past the property. He asks if I think the dogs will come out. Maybe they've died, he speculates. Perhaps they finally barked themselves to death.

A tumult of baying confirms that the dogs are very much alive.

"Rabies! Psycho!" the boychild cries, overjoyed to see the snarling faces and flashing teeth of the neighbourhood's two most demented inhabitants. Rabies, a bristling, wall-eyed border collie, rips chunks of green sacking from the fence, simultaneously barking. I am thankful for the chain-link fence, or he'd be ripping chunks of flesh from our bones. The fence rattles and clangs every time Rabies hurls himself at it. I pray that it holds.

His companion, Psycho, a smaller but equally vicious brindled mutt, barks and yelps. Whirling in frustrated circles, he promises us that he will tear us limb from limb for the crime of venturing near his territory.

The boychild laughs uproariously at the spectacle. Rabies and Psycho rip another hunk of green sacking off the fence, then focus all their pent-up rage on shredding it to pieces. Their snarls and growls fade as we progress down the hill towards the village.

We enter a cool, dim bar. The rich, earthy smell of fresh coffee fills the air, along with the irresistible aroma of hot, buttery *cornetti*.

Cups and saucers rattle and crash onto the granite-topped bar as orders are prepared. Hot steam blasts through milk with a noisy hiss.

I order my usual cappuccino; the boychild opts for *una spremuta* – freshly squeezed orange juice with a dash of lemon. We each order a *cornetto* – an Italian croissant.

The pastries offer a satisfying crunch at the first bite; the centre is warm, gooey and sweet. The strong caffeine and the sugar hit make my pulse snap and bang.

My son eyes miniature cakes in a glass-fronted display case. Tiny pastry cases are topped with glazed strawberries, blueberries, and lime-green grapes. Squares of caramel are decorated with elaborate, paper-thin whorls of chocolate. Honey-coloured cones, no longer than a finger, burst with rich, creamy filling.

Each cake is crafted with as much artistry as a royal jeweller preparing the crown of a king.

The boychild is hoping that I will let him order some treats for dessert tonight. I limit him to six. He solemnly approaches the till and orders his selection, which is boxed up and tied with a ribbon by the smiling proprietor.

Our next stop is the *vineria*. The shop is long and narrow, edged with huge stainless-steel vats. On the back wall, numerous bottles of wine are on display. I ignore the bottles. The cylindrical vats are where the real treasure lies.

I greet the owner of the store and gesture to the first vat. He bends over, fiddles with the tap at the base and pours a little into a glass tumbler. The liquid is thick, ruby-coloured with a faint scent of blackberries. I sip it, savouring its decadent heaviness. I nod to the owner.

He frowns, holds up a hand. He juts his chin towards another vat. I shrug: why not? A second tumbler is grabbed. He twists the tap, liquid gold bubbles into the glass. This wine is light and sparkly, equally delectable. I want to buy a bottle of each, but I have only brought one empty bottle with me.

"Non è un problema," the owner smiles. He unearths an empty water bottle from under the counter.

For three euro, I have two bottles of wine. The thing is, we will need to drink them quickly as their life expectancy is short in the plastic bottles. Lightheaded after sampling drinks at nine in the morning, we head home, planning to invite neighbours over to share our loot.

Company is good. It saves me from having to talk to my husband.

I ignore a thought that leaves a cold ache in the pit of my stomach. This is one of my last Saturdays in Italy.

CHAPTER 5

Boarding school, Sixth Form house, communal area. The last day of term. I am one among many parents searching fruitlessly for their children. Two lads are sprawled across a sofa, ignoring a blaring TV: extreme close-up of a snarling gangster spitting out angry rhymes. Pile of smelly, wet trainers by the doorway. Their owners were told not to traipse mud through the corridors; so, they kick them towards the shoe rack.

I give up searching. I do not want to be late for parent-teacher meetings.

Outside: earthy stink of cold mud churned up by rugby boots. A crisp packet is blown out of a bin, circles about, spirals upwards. Leafless trees drip from last night's downpour. Icy air slips down my neck. I'm tangled with handbag, scarf, notebook and pen as I struggle to zip up my coat. A group of chattering girls. Remind me, I say to them, is this the way to the hall? They nod. Thumbs up. They don't mind the wet, icy air. Waft of hot chips, vinegar from the canteen. Path submerged! Long, deep puddle. Don't want wet shoes. Skid on the boggy lawn, arms cartwheeling. Loamy smell of mud and soggy grass. Another frigid gust blasts at me. Someone's umbrella turns inside out; she clings on as if she's wrestling with a crow. Her hair steams over her face, blinding her.

Inside the hall. Hot air feels solid with noise and perspiration. A hundred voices: triumphs, disasters. Throng of bewildered parents. Searching. Where are my son's teachers? Parents queue, then sit, hunched, leaning in, desperate. What's the verdict? Angel or devil this term? Teachers: straight-backed, eyes on laptop screens. Inscrutable. Anxiety rolls around the room in waves.

My turn. A flicker in the teacher's eyes.
Contempt?
Disgust?
Fear! She is scared of me!

She launches into a defensive monologue, swivelling around the laptop so I can see her screen. Subtext: Here's the evidence. I am a good teacher. I mark your son's work. Keep records. It's not my fault his results are shit. Here are the resources I give him. His marks are still woeful.
"It's okay. He's not Einstein. Is he behaving? Polite? Is he happy?"
She blinks. Didn't expect this.

Long drive home. Fight in the car. "Must you use such bloody disgusting language?"
"But Mum! You just swore!" Deep breath in. Hold it. Grip the steering wheel. Don't have a prang just because you're upset. Exhale. "I don't mind that your marks are crap. I just want you to be happy!"

"What sort of mum doesn't care if her son's grades are crap? For fuck's sake! I need help! I actually need you to give me a kick up the arse! How can I be happy if I'm fucking well failing and you don't give a shit? You just want me to be some fucking cute, smiling puppy."

*

Drive on my own to Walton to escape accusations that have a sting of truth to them. Grim, wintry Saturday. Muddy rollers – fattened by a storm – build, swell and crash up the beach with a foamy hiss. Tide is high; waves surge right up to the promenade wall. Gulls scream in the icy wind.

Further out on the swells, resting gulls bob. They get pushed in slowly on the tide. Reaching the breakers, they panic and escape a cresting wave, a white flurry skywards. Their silhouettes wheel and screech against the grey. Obscured sun glows copper through clouds and turns the muddy water into a mosaic of pewter and glass shards. Tang of cigarette smoke being angrily sucked in by a woman in a mustard-yellow coat. Hair scraped back, hastily tied up. Had she left home in a rush? She frowns at the sea. Her jaw works as if she's chewing or gnashing her teeth – replaying an argument, perhaps. One cold hand is shoved in her pocket, the other cradles her fag.

Across the street, a biker bar. In sleepy little Walton-on-the-Naze? They are open in the morning, and they serve cups of tea, which are exorbitant. I pay up. The barman looks hungover. He scratches his bald head, which is wrapped in a bandana, then he rubs a long sketchy beard, and blinks in surprise when I say yes, I'll have it here. Gives it to me in a polystyrene cup in case I change my mind and go somewhere where I'm not such a misfit. He hands me some change. He has studded leather bangles on his wrist and chunky silver rings on his fingers; one is shaped like a skull. 'One Night in Bangkok' blares, distorted by knackered speakers. Barrels are turned into tables. The place stinks of spilt beer, even at ten in the morning. Studded leather jackets are for sale, along with an Indian chief's head-dress. I'm tempted to buy it.

At the next table, a weather-beaten old man with scraggly long grey hair is in earnest conversation with a man dressed as a cowboy. Seventies-style blue jeans, with messages handwritten all over them in marker pen. Purple waistcoat, orange cravat. Sheriff's badge. Boots. Spurs. Battered, leather cowboy hat. Eyes concealed behind shades. He sips gin and tonic from a tin.

The barman sees me looking at the purple cowboy. "Sectioned. First morning out."

I'm surprised at his sudden friendliness. "Poor chap", I say. "You think he's okay?"

Barman ponders for a moment. "Well, they let him out, but. . ." He mimes drinking. Continues: ". . .on an empty stomach. On top of meds. It'll all kick off in a bit." He pauses. I can't resist looking again.

Barman leans in conspiratorially. "He's an accountant. Last time I saw him, he came in here wearing a smart suit, clean shaven. Then he went berserk. Trashed the place." I look around. "This place?" Barman confirms with one emphatic nod; eyes wide, eyebrows up. I'm relishing the gossip, visualising the drama. Barman crooks his forefinger, a gesture to encourage me to look down, below the bar. He points to a baseball bat. "If he kicks off, I'm ready this time."

*

Risky lifestyle choices are a symptom of undiagnosed ADHD in some adults. Some get by, developing coping mechanisms. Some feel like misfits and protect themselves by self-excluding. Some fail exams. Some become increasingly less risk averse, more impulsive. Alcohol, drugs, extreme sports appeal to some.

*

Home. Something stinks, sour and burnt. A crash in the kitchen. My son is in there, frantically scooping up glass from the floor. Smoke billows from the oven.

"I roasted a chicken for you. But, how do you cook parsnips? Because I burnt them. And I broke this glass thing."

His clumsy niceness makes the tears burst out of me. I coped better when he was boiling with rage. I smear mascara onto my sleeve, peering into the smoky oven at the cremated parsnips. Tears and laughter come simultaneously.

Head down, he mutters, "Sorry I was such a dick."

I'm sorry, too. There is something I'm just not getting right. I don't want to be one of those shrieking bitch-cow mothers that drives her son to suicide, banning television, internet, football, sugar. If I try to help him with his assignments, he huffs and sighs. Snaps pencils in two.

The old question spins around in my head. Does he have learning difficulties? But he's so articulate, so sharp witted. Yet, he flakes out every time there's a test. Writes rubbish, repeats himself. Misreads questions. Pretends to feel sick.

I wonder where to turn. Hanging a label around his neck might brand him forever. I've seen a certain breed of teacher roll their eyes and sigh when they glance at a class list that contains details of a child with learning needs. Some people think that it's the fault of mums from a broken home (check – that's me) who use screens to buy a few minutes of peace (guilty as charged) and who fed their children Coco Pops endlessly in order to stave off tantrums (I've done the middle-class ex-pat version: chocolate croissants.)

His future might be hampered by the label. It's impossible to be interviewed for certain jobs with a diagnosis of learning difficulties. I imagine a series of job interviews. "But aren't people with ADHD disorganised? And yet, you are applying to be an events organiser. . ."
The army: "Excuse me? You have a condition that makes you impulsive, but you want to work with weapons? In high-risk conflict situations?" An airline pilot: "What if you forget to listen to the control tower?"

CHAPTER 6

East Anglia beach yet again. I spend a lot of time, stomping along this stretch of coast, trying to make sense of my son's unhappiness. And mine. I've been lonely since my grandmother died. At least she left her two mad terriers to me.

Clouds sag overhead, too fat and heavy to budge when a chilly breeze blows. The damp wind lifts half-hearted rollers that splurge onto the pebbles with a noise that sounds like a sigh.

I avoid the promenade, opting instead for a footpath slightly higher up, but below the level of the main road. Better view. Fewer people. Overgrown grasses fringe the path. Seeds stick to my jeans and to the dogs' coats.

The dogs stop. They gaze intently into the grassy verge. They communicate telepathically, using secret dog language. The tips of their tails quiver. One of them prepares to pounce: she perches on her hind paws for a moment before she crashes into the grass, hoping to scare some timid little creature out from its sanctuary.

A frenzy of snuffling and yipping and whining.

I pull on the double leash gently, at first, but the dogs tug back, hard. I yank them away. I don't want to be forced to deal with a half-chewed mouse. It's happened before.

In some ways, the Roman cats were easier than my grandmother's pair of mad terriers.

I don't like thinking about Rome. It's cold here, and so grey. The cats would have hated it. They were glad to be adopted by Italian friends, escaping from the electric animosity that turned our house into a warzone in those final months before our marriage finally broke apart.

On a sandy strip of beach, away from the pebbly waterline, a child is creating a sandcastle. Her thick, bobbed hair flops over her face as she leans over, absorbed in her creation. She is dressed in a swimming costume. She does not mind the chilly air and the threat of rain. The footpath peters out, forcing me down towards her and onto the prom.

I am now close enough to see that she is not a child. Her skin is leathery and wrinkled, but she moves and babbles like a baby. She wields a hefty spade, then jumps into a waist-deep hole. With fierce concentration, she narrates her process in an unintelligible prattle.

Another secret language.

She pats the edge of the hole, frowning as she tidies it up. Then she perches on the edge, legs dangling into the hole, rocking and humming in a monotone. With the back of her hand, she wipes a ribbon of drool from her chin while she surveys her work.

She is being watched by a minder. He sits on a deckchair in the door of a beach hut, reading a newspaper and sipping tea. I realise that I had slowed down and stared. I click to gain the dogs' attention, pull on their lead and move on.

The promenade slopes upwards. At the top of the rise, a five-barred metal gate is padlocked shut, blocking entry to vehicles. An anxious dad watches a little lad clambering over the closed gate instead of simply walking through the open pedestrian access to one side.

My heart lurches. That could have been my boy when he was little. Same tousled blonde hair, same football top, same exuberant energy.

Have I travelled back in time? If I have, is this a chance to reset the disasters of the past few years?

I fantasise about the possibilities that this would offer. If I could change the past, I'd need to do some uncharacteristic planning.

I decide that I will raise the child on my own. On the night when the First Wife bursts into my tiny flat in a rage, I will take control of the situation. This time I will notice my husband's – actually, her husband's – craven reaction to her pain and fury.

I gently grab her wrists, look her in the eyes and apologise. I feel the rage ebbing out from her, and I put my arms around her and tell her that from the bottom of my heart, I am sorry. Saint Me offers to go out and leave her alone to talk with her husband for an hour or so.

While I am out, Saint Me will decide to be brave and good. I will sit down drinking a strong coffee – no. Not coffee. The smell of the stuff had me vomiting uncontrollably when I was pregnant. My son hates it to this day. I will sit down drinking mineral water – because after all, I am now a saint, and I make good decisions. I eat healthy food; I drink mineral water instead of caffeine by day and wine by night, even when I am not pregnant with a married man's child.

In my daydream, I return to the flat, and I tell the First Wife that I could not live with myself knowing that I had caused this much pain. Take your husband home, I say. I will arrange to have his stuff sent there. Get counselling. Forgive each other. I promise never to speak to him again.

*

With my feet in the present, and my head in a remodelled, utopian past, I turn away from the beach. I cut across the rec towards my house. I unclip the dogs from their double leash. They hurtle after each other across the football pitch, zigzagging in a wild chase.

*

I evaluate a different reset. This time I am in Boots, buying the pregnancy test. Some students from my school are also shopping

40

there, much to my horror. I hide the pregnancy test between two pairs of tights, grabbed hastily off the nearest display.

"Hello, Miss!"

They've seen the test! Their eyes glint. They know. One of them smirks and asks, "Are you sick?"

Actually, yes. I had been feeling a suspicious nausea for days. A colleague had been eating a banana in the staff room, and revulsion made me run outside. How could anyone eat anything that was so obviously rotten? And what was wrong with the coffee today? The stench of it!

The banana was not rotten. The coffee was fine.

But I'd had a period! It had been on time, although it had been brief. And very light.

In this version of my past, I would not take the test in my flat, where he would be waiting. I would go to a friend's house and take the test there. In this life, the two blue lines would not trigger a frenzied panic. Saint Me would take time to evaluate my situation.

I would consider whether he even needed to know about the baby. I'd ask myself whether I loved him enough to raise a child with him.

In this reset, I ended the relationship. I was gentle and kind. He was relieved. He had been growing tired of my impulsiveness and my messiness. I was fed up with him groaning when he'd overeaten, farting and burping with gusto. He might look glamorous and silver haired, but the dazzle was wearing out fast.

Of course, Saint Me would have been too kind to mention his flaws. In this version of the past, we parted company without the foul quarrels and bitter recriminations that erupted a decade later in the real world.

*

41

The dogs are uncharacteristically obedient when I call them back.

They like it when I go into a dream world like this. The dogs sense Saint Me. They like her and obey her when she calls.

There will be treats when we get back home.

CHAPTER 7

Mindfulness experts teach that dwelling on regrets is toxic. We should accept the things we cannot change. Live in the now. Practise gratitude for what we have; don't waste energy on missed opportunities.

But I enjoy chewing on my regrets, dreaming about how life could have been different. Sculpting and perfecting my perfect alternate universe is balm to me. It sends me into a deep, peaceful sleep most nights.

I prefer my brave new world where a bitter divorce did not happen. There, I did not rush to marry a man two decades older than me; and I did not break up his marriage. In every imagined alternate life, I always have my son, though. And Italy. Just without the messes.

My departure from Italy was horrible. Friends melted away when my husband repeatedly and publicly accused me of cheating. A male colleague suddenly became awkward and overfriendly. Clearly, the accusations about me and the hunky drama teacher made him hope that I would oblige him, too. He would not leave me alone. I'd sit down to lunch; he would appear next to me. At every turn, he would be there, an unwelcome, embarrassing shadow.

It was not that long ago, but #metoo had not happened. He had not touched me; he had not been lewd. He just would not go away. I believed that a complaint would have sounded ridiculous.

Sleep deprived and anxious, I forgot to turn up to lessons. The last straw came when I lost an entire set of exam papers.

I resigned before they could fire me.

The deputy head took pity on me. I would get a reasonable reference from the school, she said. When I was functioning well, I was incredibly creative in the classroom. However, there was one other thing she wanted to discuss. She thought that I should set up an appointment with a new Learning Support coordinator. My son was falling apart as disastrously as me.

"Once I leave, and get to my grandmother's place in East Anglia, everything will settle," I assured her.

The doubt and pity in her eyes made me cringe. She tilted her head and tried to persuade me: "Just have a chat with Learning Support. This new coordinator is one of the best I have ever met in my entire career. We are all very worried about you. And your son. He's exhibiting—"

"Classic signs of ADHD," I finished the well-worn sentence for her. "Please stop with the ADHD diagnosis! It is not even a clinically proven condition! The poor lad is going through hell. His parents are splitting up. He's being uprooted from all his friends. Everyone wants to pump him full of some drug that has the same chemical composition as speed! He needs help, not drugs!"

*

It is true that the molecular formula of Ritalin shares part of its basic structure with amphetamines.

*

I left the deputy head's office. I think I might have slammed her door on the way out. If I did, the prospect of a reasonable reference went up in smoke at that precise moment.

At least I did not mess things up with my grandmother, who stuck by me through everything. She offered me a home and pulled strings with an old friend to get my son a place at a boarding school. Grandmother paid for everything. It was she who suggested that I send him away while my husband and I finalised the divorce.

Yet again, I chewed over the starting point: the announcement years ago, that I was having a baby, and that the child's father needed to leave his first wife. Sparks of anger still went off in my chest about being unfavourably compared to my grandmother, a comparison driven by my mother's all-consuming bitterness about being fatherless. For God's sake! My grandmother had provided a loving, secure home!

So many people had so many reasons to resent each other. It had to stop somewhere. I exhaled slowly, releasing sour air and rage.

My wonderful Grandmother had always been held up before me as a family catastrophe, a wilful harlot who deprived my mother of normality. Grandmother was cheerfully unconcerned about her reputation. She worked hard and was shrewd with money. She gambled wildly at times. She'd once lost a staggering sum of money, but eventually recouped her losses. She never complained.

Broken as I felt right then, I resolved to restore my fortunes. I decided to take an inventory of my heart. Resentment and bitterness would be cast off as liabilities; grandmother's legacy of supportiveness and compassion – priceless assets.

In many ways, boarding school was good for my son. It granted him respite from breathing in the foul air of my break-up with his father.

For the first year at his new school, he was offered counselling, as well as support for his disorganisation. Then a letter from his school's Learning Support Department arrived. Now, an email from them has appeared in my inbox.

It bewilders me that so many teachers want to attach a syndrome to a child whose life has fallen apart.

CHAPTER 8

Last night, my son went crashing upstairs to his bedroom at two in the morning. I had given up trying to persuade him to shut down his computer late the previous evening. He had somehow attached the computer to the television. His every waking hour is spent up close to the screen, absorbed in a world of explosions and shoot-outs. Occasionally, he bellows at the screen in a rage.

The first week of the holidays has been wasted behind closed curtains and screens. Trying to persuade him to take the dogs out for a walk is a battle equal in scope and fury to the wars on the TV screen.

It can't be good for him to sit in a darkened room for fourteen hours a day, blowing things up and killing imaginary villains. I sneak downstairs while he is sleeping and remove the cables from his computer.

The following noon, he rampages through my room, ripping open cupboards and ransacking drawers. He will never find those cables. His obsession with the game is no match for my obsession with trying to get him to do something about his woeful exam results. He wanted me to give him a kick up the backside, so here it is.

I don't just want him to revise endlessly, though.

"Why don't you arrange to meet some friends from school?" I ask him. "I'll drive you anywhere, or you can hop on a train to go and visit them. They are welcome here if you like."

This suggestion causes an eruption.

Has there been some drama with his friends? The more I probe, the more sullen and defensive he becomes. There is clearly a problem.

I suggest contacting former classmates from Rome. My son is resistant to this suggestion, too. Resistant is the wrong word. Enraged would be a better description for his reaction.

*

Rejection sensitivity is an extreme emotional response, triggered by a perception that the slightest criticism – a tut, an eyeroll – signifies a catastrophic break-up.

*

If only my grandmother had not died; my son would never act like this if she was around. She had the ability to soothe the most outrageous behaviour. Despite her love of wild people and parties, she was a gentle presence: kind, calm. My son is turning the home that was once a sanctuary into a horrible warzone.

I do not believe in ghosts, but it feels like she is still here, watching, not judging. Just sending waves of compassion. I try to work out what she might have done.

I approach my son's room again, feeling like Daniel going into the lion's den. Silently, I alternate between prayer and calling out to my grandmother's spirit for help.

He is flat on his bed, frowning up at the ceiling, hands clasped behind his head. He does not acknowledge my presence and ignores the tea that I put down on the cluttered bedside table next to him. The chair in his room is piled high with filthy laundry. The room reeks of dirty socks.

My grandmother would have silently tidied up the mess.

I drag a laundry basket in and start lobbing the filthy clothes into it. Half the shelves in his wardrobe are impressively tidy; tee shirts are folded crisply and stacked. The other half are an unholy tangle. My son sits up. "I got distracted midway through tidying my cupboard," he explains. I dump a clean duvet cover and sheets onto the foot of

47

his bed. He sighs and slurps at the tea. He slouches to his feet, opens a window, and yanks off the used bed linen.

Struggling not to comment on the stink and mess, I continue tidying. For such a tiny room, the task is mammoth.

Having made his bed look freakishly neat, he frowns at his bookshelf. Books, used coffee cups and scrunched up papers are piled haphazardly onto it. Some of the contents have spilt onto the floor.

"Did you get the email from school?" he asks.

I try not to panic. What now? It's the holidays! What can he have possibly done wrong during the holidays?

He explains, "It was supposed to come at the end of term, same time as my report."

Oh. That. I had deleted it when I saw that it was from Learning Support. Not this again, I had thought.

"Everyone thinks I have ADHD, Mum. Even people in my class. They made me do a questionnaire. I'm sorry, Mum. You must hate this. I'm your only kid and I'm a total frickin' mess."

My grandmother's presence seems to fill the room more than ever. I can almost hear her gently saying to me that there is something wrong here. The boy needs help, yet he is the one apologising.

I look into his mirror hanging crooked on the wall. "It's not your fault," I say. "I think we all need help." I straighten the mirror.

Just support him properly, I tell myself. Or perhaps my grandmother's spirit tells me.

*

The email is in my deleted items folder. Attached is a questionnaire. The instructions tell me to tick one of the following boxes: Yes? No? Same/better/worse than when he was little?

Symptom 1: Often fails to give close attention to details or makes careless mistakes in schoolwork, work or other activities.

Details are the problem. Details open a new universe of ideas, and my son's brain goes prancing after any detail that catches his eye. It is the big picture that he misses every time. Like those two tidy shelves in his wardrobe, surrounded by a cluttered slum.

This is not going to be straightforward. My son and I loathe yes/no questions. The grey areas, the extraneous details, enthral us. I chew a pencil as I think about the answer. My son jiggles his foot and drums his fingers in a manic rhythm on the arm of his chair.

I slam my hand down on my desk. Channelling my grandmother's tranquillity is a thing of the past, as of now.

My son freezes. He realises that the maddening rhythm was too much for me. The drumming filled up my head, my heart, my soul.

Cocking an eyebrow, I read the next question out loud: "Often fidgets with hands or feet or squirms in seat."

Grinning, he peers at the screen of my laptop: "Easily distracted by external stimuli, mum?" He drums again, his face alight as he teases me. He draws out the vowel sounds of my name: "Mu-u-um, is this questionnaire about you or me?"
I shoot back at him: "Often loses things. . ."
Rueful laughter. The saga of lost things could fill the pages of a novel longer than anything Tolstoy produced. Its sequel: Avoided Tasks and Incomplete Assignments.

The first page of the questionnaire was not written specifically for my son, but it might as well have been.

The final page contains a question asking whether my child ever ran away from home. The jovial mood evaporates.

Silently, I tick the YES column. We avoid eye contact.

*

It had been New Year's Eve. In the morning, the boychild – my son – surprised me by clumping downstairs with a bulging rucksack on his back.

(I should stop referring to him as a boychild. He towers over me. He changes lightbulbs without needing a stepladder.)

"But your dad isn't coming to collect you until this afternoon!" I exclaimed.

He informed me that his father told him to take a train to London. I quickly busied myself with the dishes to mask a flash of irritation towards my ex. Surely he could have driven down to collect his own son during the festive season! So far, he had not even sent a Christmas card, let alone a gift. Many weekend visits had been curtailed because of music commitments; increasingly, visits from father to son were being cancelled at the last minute.

My son had seemed phlegmatic about the cancellations: "At least dad's earning money."

He was obsessing about our financial position – ironic, since my grandmother's death meant that I had some savings for the first time in my life. The more we had, the more we had to lose, as far as the boychild was concerned.

My son wouldn't let me give him a lift to the train station. I wondered if he sensed that I was trying to compensate for his father's aloofness. "I need the air, anyway, Mum. I'll enjoy walking."

He hugged me clumsily, unbalanced by his heavy rucksack, then headed out. I remember being heartened by the sparkle of excitement in his eyes. He must have missed his dad more than he let on. Perhaps he was looking forward to spending time with his dad's arty crowd.

At midnight, I tried to ring to wish him a happy New Year. I didn't really expect him to hear his phone amidst the noisy celebrations. However, a faint, tinny jingle from his bedroom signalled that he had forgotten to take his phone with him. So, I couldn't even text him to wish him well.

I decided to ring the landline instead, but not until later, when I would not be intruding on the party.

I woke up late on January the first. I rang the landline as planned, but no one answered. By the third of January, I became irritated after repeatedly failing to make contact. I needed to know the arrangements for his return. Term would start soon, and he'd need to pack. Besides, I was missing my son. The house was so silent that it seemed to throb.

Outside, a flock of herring gulls made raucous shrieks. It sounded like they were swirling about, circling over the roof and quarrelling about who got which spot, or perhaps they were just laughing at a filthy herring gull joke.

What would constitute smut from a herring gull's perspective? Did you hear the one about the two males arguing over who would mate with an albatross? Rowdy cackles filled the air. Stand-up comedy. Just winging it.

The screeching cries diminished as most of the birds flew off. Gentler mewling squawks reached my ears, an intimate crooning that parents of hatchlings use to communicate with their brood. I remembered that there was a nest on a neighbour's chimney. Speckled grey chicks had caught my eye as they tottered unsteadily along the apex of the roof while parents looked on, squawking in alarm.

I can relate to their anxiety.

Finally, late on the third of January, my ex answered the phone. He sounded out of breath and told me that he'd only just got in. I asked where they had been.

Not that it was any business of mine, but New York, he snapped.

Silence while I processed this news. Deep breaths, I told myself. Don't shout.

My husband, sounding annoyed, demanded to know what I wanted. After a moment of amazed disbelief, I snapped at him that the least he could do was tell me when and where to collect my son. (I emphasised 'my'.) And in future, I shouted, please tell me when you plan to take my boy out of the country.

A long silence. I wondered if the signal had been lost.

My ex had not seen our son since November. He had cancelled the New Year's Eve arrangement. Our son was supposed to be at home with me.

By the time the police came to the house, the shakes had set in. I didn't think I'd be able to cope with the sweet tea that a police officer made for me. My stomach boiled and knotted; my throat was so tight that I could barely answer their questions coherently. I only just managed to explain about the rucksack and the excitement in his eyes.

When the police asked me for a recent photo of my son, I pulled a drawer off its runners, spilling the contents all over the floor in a heap. Suddenly, I could not for the life of me remember the pass code to my phone. I ripped my sweater off as beads of sweat prickled my forehead. I kept telling myself that this would be a bad moment to throw up. The policewoman encouraged me to sit down. My pulse was roaring in my ears.

I had already endured questions that were laden with a hideous subtext: exactly how messed up a parent are you to have provoked your son to disappear? Are you abusive? May we look in his bedroom (to search for drugs paraphernalia, perhaps)?

I sat staring at my feet as I focused every ounce of strength on not vomiting. What sort of mother could not dig deep and provide helpful information? I was useless!

And now all I could do was wallow in self-pity, crippled with fear.

There was a tornado of questions whirling in my skull: Is he alive? Should I have insisted that his dad visited more often? Am I such an awful mother that my son ran away? Were there any signs that this was coming? Yes! No, perhaps not. Where is he? Is there a mystery girlfriend or boyfriend that I know nothing about? Might he be with him or her? Has he joined a cult? Don't be ridiculous! Is he alive? I'd know if he wasn't! He is alive! Is he injured?

My ex-husband arrived looking old and dishevelled. I steeled myself for a barrage of accusations from him. I needn't have. He moved slowly but purposefully, producing recent photos of our son, and reminding me of my pin code for my phone. It had remained unchanged since our marriage. The photos were circulated to patrolling police cars and the coast guard.

Our son was found six hours later, wandering along the sea front miles up the coast. After sleeping rough for three nights in freezing rain and wind, he was showing signs of illness setting in. He'd taken no money with him; he was hungry and badly dehydrated. His backpack had been stolen from him while he slept fitfully one night. He was kept in hospital for a few hours under observation, rehydrated on a drip, then sent home with antibiotics.

We had expected a flurry of visits from social services, but the whole event seemed to fizzle. The police and medical experts dismissed our son as just another silly kid.

He explained that he wanted to prove that he could stand on his own two feet in the wild. My husband and I gaped at him. East coast seaside towns aren't much of a wilderness, but we supposed that he had successfully run the gauntlet of drunken revellers, vicious stray cats, and wild-eyed homeless chaps in stinking alleyways.

His father was reluctant to return to London. He was dithering about awkwardly, trying to be helpful in the kitchen when he asked if I thought we should try to repair our relationship, try again. He looked relieved when I said no. But it was nice that hostilities were suspended.

CHAPTER 9

It has been a year since treatment and counselling began. Because he was over the age of sixteen, we had to use a private clinic. My grandmother's legacy meant that we could afford to pay. I'd still have preferred to have her here with us, rather than her money.

My son's father met us at the clinic for the first appointment. I was glad that he was there. He had stopped cancelling visits after my son ran away. These days, he comes to every appointment, listening intently and writing notes.

That first time, we had sat in the waiting room, unable to read or talk, watching the minutes pass by before we could join my son and the psychiatrist. We were going to hear about the results of tests that had been carried out in the preceding weeks. The waiting room had an eerie silence to it. The light was dim and blue in the early morning.

Behind a closed door, our son was being seen. It was hard not to worry about what was being said behind that door, or what was being done. A picture kept popping into my mind of my son connected to electrodes and heart monitors – how I wished I had previously conducted some research about how ADHD is diagnosed.

I had never visited a psychiatrist before. I wondered who else had sat in this waiting room and why.

The psychiatrist summoned us. She reminded me of a little bird. She had bright eyes and moved with quick, light steps. She was reassuringly calm and intensely alert at the same time. My son, looking relaxed, sat waiting for us in her office. There were no signs of any suspicious wires, machines, or needles.

The psychiatrist patted a folder. She explained that it contained a detailed report, compiled after she assessed my son by asking him a series of questions. Earlier, at school, his teachers had responded to questionnaires that helped inform the diagnosis. Additionally, some cognitive ability tests had been carried out.

It was obvious that she had warmed to my son, as many had throughout his life. That had always been a feature: when and if people connected with him, it was hard to dislike his mischievous humour and his curiosity.

The psychiatrist confirmed that my son certainly had ADD, which is treated in the same way as ADHD. Without hyperactivity, the condition is harder to spot. Prior to diagnosis, a child with ADD can be branded lazy, inattentive, or disorganised. The impact of this on self-esteem can lead to depression and anxiety.

She reassured my ex-husband and me that treatment would reduce the lapses in attention. Counselling would enable him to manage the condition, and medication would increase the concentration of neurotransmitters that control reasoning and help my son to manage his executive function skill.

"What are executive function skills?" My husband spoke up for the first time.
"The ability to tune out distractions. In fact, many medical practitioners have stopped calling the condition 'Attention Deficit Hyperactive Disorder'. The ability to hyperfocus makes 'attention deficit' a misnomer."
"What do they call it instead?" my son asked.
The inevitable acronym was supplied: "EFDD. Executive Function Developmental Delay."
My ex shrugged. "I suppose a developmental delay is an easier label to carry than a deficit. Implies there's hope that he can sort it out one day. Better late than never."

The psychiatrist chewed the end of her pen for a moment. I wondered what she thought about my husband's comment.

My son took advantage of the pause, and asked, "Can you help me start giving a damn about what I'm meant to be doing? Because, at the moment, I know I should care about deadlines and essays, but I just shelve them. I stop caring at the crucial moment."

I frowned. Everyone procrastinates. I was uncomfortable about the medicalisation of a normal adolescent tendency.

But then, my son continued: "I feel as if there is a wheel inside my skull. The stuff I need to access is all there on that wheel. But I just can't stop the wheel spinning at the right moment!"
"So, you can't access the specific knowledge you need at the right time and place?" the psychiatrist asked.
"Exactly. I walk out of exams and tests, then half an hour later I remember what I should've written."

Normal enough for most people sometimes, but this was my son's experience all the time. . . and not just in tests. In debates, conversations and arguments, his mind would spin uncontrollably until intense hyperfocus set in —usually on the wrong topic.

"So, people think I'm just thick." He sagged as he said it. "And I am a bit. But I'm not as stupid as they think. I just can't get the words out in time. I'm not quick enough."

I reached out and squeezed his hand.

As the psychiatrist opened the file, she cautioned us that the tests were a standardised means of measuring abilities. They were imperfect in many ways, but useful for providing a baseline to help clients understand themselves. She scanned the sheafs of papers and told us that his numeric ability, when compared to students of similar age and educational background, was somewhat below average. However, linguistically he was off the charts. He was in the ninety-ninth percentile, meaning that his verbal ability made him exceptionally gifted! It was just that he was not able to shine because his processing skills were impeded by his condition.

"I'm clever enough to know when I'm being dumb!" My son started laughing ruefully.

The psychiatrist put her head to one side and smiled gently at him, "It's time to stop using words like 'dumb' when you talk about yourself. All your life, you have worked twice as hard as most of your classmates, just to keep up. The fact that you've coped comparatively well tells me that you are remarkable."

My son lifted his chin. He stared at the psychiatrist, his face alight with amazement.

She continued: "You really do have masses of potential. With support, you could thrive in an academic setting if you so choose. Do remember, however, that academic success is not the only measure of success in the world."

He brushed his eyes roughly. I also felt my throat tightening. Her positive affirmation was like a fragile, beautiful creature that had just landed in the room. It could shatter and be lost forever with the slightest wrong move or word.

Before continuing, she paused, letting us digest her words before moving on. She recommended that he start on a low dose of medication. The GP would monitor him carefully. I was thankful that the medical centre at his boarding school would supervise regular dosage as I was terrified that I would forget.

The psychiatrist paused for a moment before her quick, dark eyes focused on me. "The condition often runs in families."

Surely not? I am nothing like my son! I do forget some things sometimes. Well, quite a lot. I do become completely engrossed in things that interest me, but that's normal! It is not the same as hyperfocus, is it? I have struggled all my life with organisation, but that's normal for a busy working mum. Well, for some busy working mums. I do seem to be conspicuously disorganised. . . But I don't have ADHD! Or EFDD, or anything!

My ex-husband smiled at the psychiatrist.

*

That was a year ago.

Now, I stand in front of my grandmother's house, which is completely empty. The roses that she had planted in the front garden are weighed down with blooms. Bees zigzag from blossom to blossom, slowly becoming inebriated on their heady perfume and sweet nectar.

In ancient times, people believed that bees, symbols of industry and perseverance, carried messages from the divine.

The removal van had driven away moments earlier; my son and I stood outside, staring after it. We needed a moment before being able to face the empty house.

Until recently, the thought of letting this house go, even temporarily, was unbearable. I had not realised that it had been my North Star for most of my life.

*

I had once heard a story about a man on the Titanic who hastily crammed money and a few precious possessions into a holdall. As the ship was sinking, he had to leap for a life raft. Prior to jumping, a crew member yelled "Let it go!".

The man would not let his holdall go. He leapt, clutching the small, but bulky bag to his chest. He overbalanced, missed the raft and splashed into the icy water. Kicking furiously, he tried to reach the raft where people stretched their hands out towards him.

The air had been punched out of his lungs by the iciness of the sea. He was shocked at how swiftly his limbs became deadened by the biting chill. The cold entered deep into him, all the way to his veins.

Still, the man clung onto his bag. He forced himself to kick and kick. When he was close enough to the raft, he tried to swing his holdall to the outstretched hands. The effort pushed him right under the surface for a moment. But someone managed to lean perilously far out from the life raft, gripped him by the hair and pulled him back up, just far enough to be enable him to take a deep, ragged gasp for breath. Choking and spluttering, he grew even weaker within seconds. Again, he heaved his waterlogged, weighty holdall, but was unable to haul it clear of the water.

"Let it go!" the people on the life raft screamed.

In some versions of the story, the man let go, was hauled aboard, and lived. In others, his possessions dragged him down.

*

I had decided to let go of my grandmother's property. Not forever. I would rent it out, initially for one year. I would also let my son go. Just for a bit. Long enough to help us both survive.

*

My son hoisted his new rucksack onto his shoulders. At his feet lay another smaller bag, crammed with books.

"Are you sure you have enough money?" I asked yet again.

He wasn't listening. He was intently watching a car turning into our close.
"It's dad! He's on time!"

Still, I fussed. "Have you got your meds? And did you take today's dose?"

He had. We both obsessively referred to an online calendar. Without it, well — we had grim memories of missed assignments and lost exam papers.

Renaissance artists placed pictures of skulls in corners of their works: *memento mori*. A chilling reminder that one day, we will perish. Be humble, the skulls tell us. Remember, one day, you will die. You're only human.

I had obsessively placed post-it notes all over the house. The notes said, look at your calendar, every day, several times a day. You're only human, and extremely forgetful. I called them my *memento forgetti*.

*

My ex-husband climbed out of his new car – a symbol of his burgeoning success as a musician. I was pleased for him and crooned over the car's sleek black paintwork and leather seats. Secretly, I thought it looked like a hearse.

"Do you need a lift anywhere?" he asked me.

I'd made my own plans. I did not want to distract him from the task of setting my son on track for his gap year. "When will his tuition start?" I asked my ex. My son would spend three months intensively studying subjects he'd failed at school, ready to do resits. His gap year would start with gap-filling.

"I'll miss you, mum," he said, hugging me. I knew he wasn't just saying it to help me feel better: he would not be able to charm his way out of onerous tasks when his father was supervising. Intensive studying would be hard, even with the help of medication and his father's orderly routine in London.

"I'll miss you too. But you will have an amazing time. Well, you will once you finish the resits. Just don't lose that email with the link to your plane tickets and paperwork for your Zambian gap year placement. You will have a great time in Africa. Try to come back in one piece. Don't head off without that first aid kit that I prepared for you."

I managed to hold back the tears until the car disappeared.

My taxi pulled up. I wiped my eyes, retrieved my little rucksack from the house, locked up and whispered a silent blessing on the place that had been my anchor.

"Stansted Airport is it, love?" the taxi driver called, one elbow propped in the window. "Blimey, you travel light, don't you? Just that one tiny bag! Wish my missus could do that. Spent a fortune on excess baggage last time we was heading off."

He kept a stream of friendly banter flowing while I sorted out my seatbelt. On my lap was a manila folder containing my paperwork: passport, print-out of the air ticket, rental agreement, employment contract.

"So, where you headed?" he asked. "Anywhere nice? Somewhere with a bit of sunshine?"

The tight knot between my shoulder blades softened. I leaned back in my seat, luxuriating in the lightness and warmth that started to wash through me.
"Italy," I said. "I'm moving back to Italy."

THREE DEMONS – A SHORT STORY

All their lives, Umberto and his ageing group of pals would meet at Pietro's Bar-Ristorante for a late Saturday breakfast and gossip. They would enjoy strong, aromatic coffee while admiring the views onto Lake Bracciano glittering in the sunshine. On this particular day, Umberto carefully wiped his mouth with a pristine table napkin before leaving it folded neatly next to his plate. He thanked the waitress clearing his table, before asking after her family. Behind the bar, Pietro, the owner, blasted steam through milk with an explosive hiss of the coffee machine, clattering spoons and cups as he kept up with the orders.

The lazy breakfast had lasted beyond lunchtime; now Umberto needed to head home to his modest villa nearby. He tapped his watch, indicating to his grandson that it was time to go.

Umberto found his walking stick, placed his panama hat on his snowy hair and called out an amiable goodbye to everyone in the bar, dropping a couple of coins onto the table. Soon, the bar would close for a few hours: the hottest part of the day was approaching.

He and Antonio, his grandson, exited through the glass door and followed a flower-lined path towards the promenade that curved around the edge of the lake. The sultry June heat made them grateful for the shade provided by tall umbrella pines. Cicadas chirruped hypnotically. Only a handful of lakeside businesses remained open, selling ice-creams to sweaty tourists.

"Nonno, may I ask you something?" Antonio asked. Even as a gangly fifteen-year old with a tendency to surliness, Antonio's affection and respect for his grandfather remained absolute.

Umberto had been waiting for this. He had sensed that his grandson was troubled. Antonio took a deep breath, thankful to be able to confide in his grandfather without fear of being teased. He unburdened himself, explaining that he was in love with a girl in his class. His feelings were not reciprocated. She preferred Antonio's athletic, tall friend. Jealousy and misery twisted Antonio's face as he complained.

Ah, thought Umberto. It is time. I need to warn the boy. He is so like me in so many ways. He needs to learn to master his passions before they master him. Umberto took a short detour away from the promenade and used his stick to point up a steep, narrow street; a stark contrast to the pretty lakefront. Cars were parked on either side, crammed in with only millimetres to spare between each bumper and partially obstructing the dogshit-encrusted pavements. Suffocating heat radiated off the buildings.

"This is where one of the most humiliating experiences of my life began, Antonio. I used to live in that apartment, there, with my Mama, right up until her death."

Antonio gaped. His grandfather had always seemed so polished, so genteel. It was hard to imagine him anywhere other than in his gracious villa overlooking the lake, with its elegant, well-tended gardens. His Nonno would have been so out of place living here, in a drab street lined with boxy apartment buildings, better suited to lonely pensioners or unhappy divorcees trying to make do on a meagre budget.

"One day, when I was no more than twenty-five – it must have been August because the heat was like an inferno – a new neighbour was moving into the long-empty apartment upstairs. When I saw her, it was love at first sight."

64

Old Umberto's eyes twinkled lasciviously for a split second as he described the young woman to his teenaged grandson, who laughed, amazed at the idea of his courteous, white-haired grandfather as a young, hot-blooded man. "Cecilia was her name. Oh, mama mia - she wore the shortest skirt and had the longest silky hair. A welcome sight compared to the usual downtrodden residents here."

Umberto gazed up the street, remembering his infatuation. He must have been standing in her way, he thought, blocking her passage up the steps to the apartment as she struggled with a hefty box. "*Pezzo di merda!*" She had sworn while he stood there, spellbound.

He tried to help, noticing how the heavy box was slowly slipping from her grasp. He accidentally brushed her arm as he tried to lift the burden from her. That touch had felt like ten thousand volts of pure, magical electricity, making him gasp and drop the box.

Even now, decades later, Umberto felt crushed with embarrassment, remembering what a clumsy buffoon he had been.

He told his grandson about the crash of plates onto polished granite steps and Cecilia's cry of despair. What a fool he must have looked! Operatic-scale rage had been unleashed: she screamed and ranted. Replacing her destroyed crockery would be an unwelcome expense.

"But obviously you paid to replace the plates?" Antonio asked. His Nonno was such a stickler for form, for putting things right.

Umberto shook his head. "To my great shame, it did not occur to me. You see, *carissimo*, there was no money, and I do not mind admitting to you that I had no brains, either. I spent my youth dogged by three demons: ignorance, poverty and my father."

Antonio was faintly aware that money had been scarce when his

Nonno was a boy, but poverty was a word that shocked him. As for ignorance – Nonno was obsessed with education; surely, he had never been ignorant?

"It is a hot day. Let us find somewhere cool to sit down, while I explain to you. My long story might help you to cope with your thwarted romance at school."

Umberto recounted how he had been born to parents who were struggling in the poverty that beset Italy after the war. His father was a loud-mouthed bully who wondered if it had been such a good idea to topple Mussolini because of the hopeless struggle to find work and feed his family in the miserable post-war climate. In the poky apartment, Umberto's father kept a huge, moth-eaten tricolour flag displayed proudly over a cluttered mantelpiece. In its centre was an angry, black eagle clutching a bundle of sticks in its claws.

"Mama and I cowered in fear of my father, like dogs," Umberto told Antonio. "Beatings were frequent but unpredictable. However, on my ninth birthday, everything changed."

His father had failed to return home from a day of casual work. An anxious evening was spent waiting, not daring to eat the birthday dinner before the man of the house came home.

A visit from the Carabinieri felt like the best birthday present that Umberto could have wished for. His father had been killed in a bar room brawl. It would not be worth pressing charges: his father was the aggressor. When the police departed, mother and son dropped all pretence of shock and grief.

Wordlessly, Umberto's mother waddled over to the flag, tugged hard at one corner and ripped it down. She shuffled with it crumpled in her hands and threw it into the trash. Together, they sat and devoured every morsel of the birthday meal. The food, seasoned with liberation, tasted better than anything they had ever eaten in their lives.

Umberto explained to his grandson that academic failure was inevitable after years of living in constant fear of his father's violence. Beatings had reduced the young Umberto a trembling shadow. His father had always been frustrated that Umberto was not manly enough, not a bloodthirsty, vengeful firebrand; so, he beat the wits out of the child. Teachers were no help: they merely became exasperated with his inability to master the basics of reading, writing or mathematics. Once freed from his domineering father, Umberto adopted the role of class clown. Many of his classmates mocked him; some pitied him.

Despite Antonio's adoration of his grandfather and surprise at his revelations, he was growing impatient. How was an abusive great-grandfather, long dead, supposed to help him solve his romantic troubles? Umberto's eyes twinkled with amusement. He recognised his grandson's impatience – so like himself as a young man; thankfully, without the thick veneer of foolishness and wilful ignorance that Umberto had once coated over himself.

"When that pretty girl moved into the apartment upstairs," Umberto told his grandson, finally gaining the boy's full attention, "it felt like the answer to my mother's prayers. I was in my mid-twenties, just about old enough to marry. My Mama had no grip on reality – she filled her head with syrupy romances and nonsense. I had no serious job. I took temporary labouring jobs wherever I could – but only if I fancied them. I would never have been able to support a wife. I was lazy, ignorant and terribly fat. I tried to eat my way out of my troubles!"

Yet, egged on by his Mama, Umberto's infatuation for Cecilia grew. But Umberto seemed to be invisible to Cecilia, despite their disastrous first encounter. She was deaf to his greetings. Regardless, Umberto trailed after Cecilia whenever he could. He invented ludicrous excuses to appear in the same coffee shops and grocery stores as her. She was oblivious to his attention. Little did he realise at the time that she was preoccupied with planning how to capture the heart of a handsome colleague, an Englishman, who was teaching with her in a nearby school.

Umberto confessed to his grandson that he would listen breathlessly for the sound of Cecilia's footsteps in her apartment upstairs when she was home. When she was away teaching, he would rave about her to anyone who had the time and patience to listen. He had convinced himself that love was mutual and devout. There were signs that he considered undeniable.

"She is shy, but she is sending tiny signals," he earnestly explained to his group of pals enjoying their usual breakfast together.

He remembered how this was met with a mix of incredulous jeering and some concern.

Pietro, the proprietor, had tried to warn Umberto that Cecilia was just another fantasy. Since their schooldays together, Pietro had tried to dissuade Umberto from falling in love with long-haired, petite girls with scornful, flashing eyes; none of them ever loved Umberto back.

Umberto argued, "She leaves the light on in the stairwell leading up to her apartment. She knows that the light drives my Mama crazy - it disturbs Mama's sleep; she knows that I must come out and switch it off."

"But Umberto, she has never met your Mama! How could she know such a thing?"

"You will see. She is crazy about me. She is the one. There will be little baby Umbertos all over the piazza this time next year."

"Umberto, you are optimistic about many things, including the number of babies that a woman can produce in one year!"

"I love her so much that she will have twins! Triplets, even!"

The laughter faded from old Umberto's face when he moved his narrative on to a darker chapter.

He described one particular Saturday morning. He was in Pietro's unusually early. He had been out all night, working as a temporary labourer, repairing a nearby road. Cecilia sashayed into Pietro's, her long, glossy hair rippling down her back. Umberto's heart fluttered. For a split second, he was convinced that he was the reason for her to choose this, his favourite bar, for her morning cappuccino. But his joy was short-lived. Behind Cecilia came a tall, blonde-haired Englishman with ice-blue eyes and a satisfied smirk on his lips. The earliness of the hour and the smouldering glances between the couple suggested that Cecilia had spent an enjoyable, sleepless night with her handsome colleague.

The lakeside restaurant was a romantic place for breakfast, Umberto supposed. The whitewashed bar-ristorante overlooked the vivid sapphire Lake Bracciano, with mulberry-red bougainvillea growing up its walls and onto the low roof. It was probably becoming very easy for the English teacher to forget the damp air, grey skies and greasy cafés of his home as he admired the view through wide open windows that let in the cooling breeze. It was already hot outside, despite the earliness of the hour.

Anxiously, Pietro had scurried over to Umberto, suspecting that exhaustion and jealousy might result in a drama. Pietro hoped that the large brandy he had hastily poured for Umberto would soothe him: he was visibly tormented by the sight of Cecilia and her lover flirting, touching at any excuse. Umberto's hands were clenched to stop them from shaking. Pietro placed his arm around his stricken friend.

Cecilia clearly had not noticed her neighbour; if she had, she did not recognise him. Much to the waitress's consternation, Pietro ordered a second triple brandy for Umberto, who downed it in a swift, angry gulp. A third large brandy was ordered, and was sipped more slowly, Umberto's trembling hands making the liquid slop over the lip of the glass.

Umberto recalled how he had glared at Cecilia and her lover smiling into each other's eyes. Their hunger for each other was undeniable. He felt as if a match was being lit somewhere deep in his chest; sparks of misery and envy smouldered uncomfortably.

"All my life, I had doused such sparks because I did not wish to be anything like my vicious father with his frightening outbursts of rage."

That time, however, the ghost of his hot-tempered father loomed in Umberto's mind.

"'Blood and honour! Blood and honour, my son,' my father used to shout at me," Umberto said, recalling his father's steely eyes glaring into his frightened face. "I was just a little boy. What was honour? And didn't blood mean pain?" But on that long-ago Saturday, Umberto started groping blindly towards understanding. In a fog of painful humiliation and rejection, the word "honour" came to him. This is a matter of honour, he decided as brandy and envy burned inside him, corroding the humour and optimism from his big, foolish heart.

Young Antonio hung his head: his grandfather's next words would echo precisely how he was feeling about his unrequited love at school. Does she not understand how happy I will make her? Why does she prefer that big *straniero,* with his stupid blonde hair and blue eyes?

Umberto recalled how he had been forced, there and then, to accept that Cecilia had not ever loved him. Memories of being scoffed at and rejected by every girl that he had ever liked flooded back. He could no longer cover up his misery and embarrassment with a clownish veneer of laughter and foolishness. Umberto's humiliation and anger boiled in his chest; his blood pounded in his ears. His fantasy had been utterly destroyed by this big, blonde foreigner, putting his hands all over the woman that he had believed was his destiny. How the thought had sickened him! Breathing hoarsely, Umberto clenched his fist and brought it crashing down onto the table, again and again.

"I wished the surface of that table was that smug bastard's face," Umberto told his amazed grandson. "Everything seemed to conspire to humiliate and frustrate me. I could not even stand up to leave! My fat belly trapped me between the table and the wall."

Pietro must have been off serving customers at this point, not realising that the effect of the early morning alcohol on Umberto's empty stomach was the precise opposite to what he had intended. Far from being soothed by the brandy, Umberto slipped his hands under the table, palms up, and with one mighty heave, up-ended it. Glasses and china crashed to the floor, shattering.

"I wanted that man dead, Antonio," Umberto admitted, squirming a little as he replayed the scene in his mind. Unsteadily,

71

he had bent down and picked up a large, jagged shard of broken crockery. He waved the sharp-edged fragment of broken plate, blood seeping through his fingers where it cut into his hand gripping it hard. He didn't feel any pain. His right hand still bore the livid scars to this day, five decades after the event, so deep had the cuts been.

Umberto made his way unsteadily across the bar towards the Englishman. Remembering the way the surprised man sat transfixed, staring at him, Umberto supposed he must have looked deranged, staggering and wild with envy. He lunged at his rival, who leapt out of his chair, tipping it over backwards. No one else in the restaurant moved. Perhaps no one believed that the lunge towards the English teacher was the precursor to a serious attack. But the attack came, with the Englishman stumbling backwards, throwing empty chairs in the path of his aggressor. On the his victim's face was a look of horrified disbelief.

The Englishman edged backwards towards the door, Umberto repeatedly lunging at him with the pointed fragment of china, wielding it like a blade. Droplets of blood sprayed from his wounded hand every time he stabbed at the air, feinting horribly close to the face of his rival, whose only option was to race outside. The restaurant was in complete disarray: smashed plates, overturned chairs. It had been reduced to chaos in a few seconds.

"Once outside, I pursued him. If I had not been so drunk and so exhausted from working all night, I swear I would have killed him," Umberto told his spellbound grandson. "But the Englishman kept turning around, allowing me to get nearer. I guess he was unable to believe that the whole scene was not a nightmare."

Pietro, the bar owner, who had been rooted to the spot with horror, had finally come to his senses and raced out after his friend, grabbed him and tried to make him see reason. "But I pushed Pietro aside and charged at the Englishman. I had murder in my heart. I wanted to sink that sharp-edged fragment into his neck and gouge out his eyes."

"My God, Nonno! What happened next?"

"Utter humiliation. Pietro, the Englishman and even Cecilia, all overpowered me simultaneously. I crashed down, falling onto the terracotta path outside the restaurant. I banged my head on the corner of a concrete flower pot filled with geraniums. It broke. I lay there, stupefied, lying on the path, with broken geraniums on my head like the crown of a fool."

Umberto passed out on the pathway, bleeding profusely from a gash to the back of his skull, three inches across. As consciousness returned, Umberto stared at the faces looking anxiously down at him. He moaned between laboured, rattling breaths. He saw the scorn in Cecilia's eyes, a look he recognised. He'd seen it before in the eyes of previous objects of his infatuation: scorn, fear, disgust.

Umberto permitted himself to see how others saw him: a hot-headed fool who was going to end up just like his father, dying ignominiously, defeated after a drunken brawl that was entirely of his own making. The clenching, suffocating agony of self-loathing was far more painful than his physical wounds. He knew that his life choices so far had been dictated by those three crushing, humiliating demons: his abusive father, ignorance and poverty.

Umberto's avoidance of a prison sentence was tribute to string-pulling by Pietro, who had looked out for him since they had been schoolboys together. Additionally, the magistrate and the Carabinieri, who had known and liked Umberto all their lives, let him off with a reprimand. A long stint in hospital was unavoidable, however.

With his mother weeping and fussing by his bedside, Umberto had time to reflect. As he slowly recovered from his head injury, he resolved to catch up on his education. Never again would he be looked at with such contempt, he decided. With the single-minded dedication he had once used for causing chaos in school and making peers laugh, Umberto now devoted himself to serious reading. Slowly, stumbling through texts, Umberto wrestled and struggled with words and concepts, discreetly receiving help from Pietro.

When his physical strength permitted, he worked as a labourer on a building site, arriving early and leaving late every day.

Umberto strove hard to change from the boorish twenty-five year old he had once been, educating himself, labouring diligently, mastering skills as a builder. His muscles hardened and his mind sharpened; his manners improved as he studied the habits and dress of the wealthy, fashionable Romans who spent their weekends in the pretty lakeside town.

Within a decade, Umberto had learnt book-keeping and was ready to launch his own construction business. Fathers began pushing their daughters towards him in the hope that he would marry one of them — this was still in the days when a desirable match meant everything. Umberto resisted. He would not look at another woman until he had conquered his demons. Only when he was almost forty, did Umberto settle with a kind-hearted, brilliant doctor with thick glasses, wiry hair and a warm smile. They enjoyed a true partnership, loving, respectful, affectionate.

Umberto sometimes spotted the Englishman and Cecilia glancing nervously over their shoulders at him, the lunatic who had once launched a random attack on them. When the couple married, they

74

received an anonymous gift of expensive plates from an exclusive store in Rome. They never guessed who sent them.

Concluding his story to his grandson, Umberto lifted a tress of snowy hair, revealing a three-inch scar on the back of his head. The boy sat round-eyed, trying to visualise his sweet-tempered, wise grandfather as the village idiot with an uncontrollable temper. His respect for his grandfather burgeoned. He had conquered such demons, overcome such humiliation. Antonio was ready to do battle with his own demon, now. No matter how hard ithe fight might prove to be, he would no longer give in to envy.

He smiled at his wise grandfather reaching for his walking stick, cautioning, "Jealousy nearly destroyed me, my boy. Let her go."

ACKNOWLEDGEMENTS

Firstly, Matthew de Abaitua, outstanding lecturer in creative writing at Univerisity of Essex, set the ball rolling with his MA assignments. His eagle eye for detail both terrified and inspired me.

Also, heartfelt thanks to my patient first readers and critics, Lily Lawes, Stanley Kenani, and my long-suffering husband, Robert (who in no way, shape or form resembles the appalling characters in either story.)

Maria Radford, motivator and encourager from the outset, along with Rebekah Stamps and Dani French, advised me about the tone of the scene with the psychiatrist of the "normal boy" .

Alex Mackenzie, the greatest editor in the world, edited and tweaked *Just a Normal Boy*. Her professionalism, humour and support kept me going and forced me to raise my game.

To the hundreds of ADHD kids who have crossed my path, including my own, thank you. Lyn McIlwaine, you helped us so much, diagnosing the condition and giving us the courage to look in the mirror.

Just a Normal Boy originally featured a combination of my own children, but the Boychild quickly took on a life and personality of his own. He is fictional. Almost.

Inspiration to write tightly-structured, snappy, patchwork prose came from the incomparable writer, Jenny Offhill. In her novella, *Dept of Speculation*, she mentioned "art monsters", a creature that I wish I could be. Likewise, author Deborah Levy unknowlingly encouraged me to face "things I don't want to know".

The attack in "Three Demons" really happened; but the background and characters are pure imagination. I hope that the attacker found the peace and tranquillity that Umberto enjoyed in the end.

ABOUT THE AUTHOR

Petrina McGregor

Petrina began writing in earnest in her fifties after completing a creative writing course at the University of Essex. There, she received guidance and encouragement, taking inspiration from writers such as Jenny Offill and Deborah Levy.

She has taught in the UK and abroad for many years, and lives in Essex.